THE CAMP KNOCK KNOCK MYSTERY

Betsy Duffey

illustrated by Fiona Dunbar

Published by
Bantam Doubleday Dell Publishing Group, Inc.
1540 Broadway
New York, New York 10036

Text copyright © 1997 by Betsy Duffey
Illustrations copyright © 1997 by Fiona Dunbar
All rights reserved.

Library of Congress Cataloging-in-Publication Data
Duffey, Betsy.
    The Camp Knock Knock mystery / Betsy Duffey : illustrated by Fiona
Dunbar.
        p.   cm.
    "A Yearling first choice chapter book."
    Sequel to: Camp Knock Knock.
    Summary: If Willie will change into clean clothes while at summer camp,
he may find the joke book which Crow has hidden from him.
    ISBN 0-385-32301-8 (hardcover : alk. paper). –ISBN 0-440-41310-9
(pbk. : alk. paper)
    [1. Jokes–Fiction.   2. Camps–Fiction.]   I. Dunbar, Fiona, ill.   II. Title.
PZ7.D896Can   1997
[E]–dc20   96-16071
                                                                   CIP
                                                                   AC

Hardcover: The trademark Delacorte Press® is registered in the U.S.
Patent and Trademark Office and in other countries.
Paperback: The trademark Yearling® is registered in the U.S. Patent and
Trademark Office and in other countries.
The text of this book is set in 17-point Baskerville.
Manufactured in the United States of America
July 1997
10 9 8 7 6 5 4 3 2 1

Contents

1. Secret Weapon

"Knock knock."

Willie was back at camp.

"Who's there?" the campers yelled.

Willie was the knock-knock king.

He knew the best jokes.

"Ivan," Willie called.

"Ivan who?" they shouted back.

A big boy jumped in front of Willie.

"Ivan to bite your neck!" he said.

"Crow!" Willie frowned.

"That was my joke!"

Crow just laughed.

"Last year you were the king," he said.

"This year I will get you back."

Mr. Harry blew the whistle.

The kids got in a line.

The parents got ready to leave.

"Mr. Harry," Willie's mother said.

"Make sure Willie changes his clothes.

Last year his trunk was never opened!"

"Mr. Harry," Slug's father said.

"Slug must read at least one book."

"Mr. Harry," Crow's mother said.

"Do not let Crow eat too much pie."

At last the parents left.

9

Mr. Harry blew the whistle.

"Another week at camp is here.

Ah, nature!" he said.

He put his hand on his heart.

He looked up at the mountains.

"Back to the singing of the birds.

Back to the call of the tree toad.

Right, campers?" he asked.

There was no answer.

The campers were gone.

They were already back to having fun.

Slug and Willie walked to their cabin.

"Are you worried about Crow?"

Slug asked.

Willie shook his head.

He patted his backpack.

"I have a secret weapon."

"What's the secret weapon?"

"A book."

"A book?"

Willie nodded.

"A book of knock-knock jokes!
Now I will know more jokes than Crow."

"Great!" Slug said. "Show me."

Willie opened his backpack.

The secret weapon was gone!

They looked at each other.

They said one word.

"Crow!"

2. Joke Talk

Willie and Slug ran to find Crow.

Crow was already up to his tricks.

He had Mr. Harry's underwear.

He was putting it up the flagpole.

"Knock knock," Crow said.

"Give me back my book," Willie said.

"Knock knock," Crow said again.

The underwear was going up.

A boy named Tim stood beside Crow.

"He will only talk in jokes," Tim said.

"Oh, all right," Willie said.

"Who's there?" he asked Crow.

"Izzy."

"Izzy who?"

"Izzy mad because I took his book?"

"Yes!" said Slug.

Crow just smiled.

He left to play another trick.

Willie and Slug followed him.

Crow climbed up a pole to a big bell.

The bell would wake them up.

Crow taped it so that it couldn't ring.

He got down.

Willie was waiting for him.

"Knock knock," Willie said.

"Who's there?" Crow asked.

"Batter."

18

"Batter who?"

"Batter tell me where my book is!"

Crow just laughed and walked away.

This time he went to the bathrooms.

He hid all the toilet paper.

"Knock knock," Crow said to Willie.

"Who's there?"

"Jess."

"Jess who?"

"Jess read the clues to find the book."

"Clues!" said Slug. "What clues?"

Crow just smiled again.

"Knock knock," he said.

"Who's there?" Willie asked.

"Dishes."

"Dishes who?"

"Dishes the Camp Knock Knock mystery." Crow laughed.

Willie put his hands on his hips.

"Knock knock," he said.

"Who's there?" Crow asked.

"Emma."

"Emma who?"

"Emma knock-knock king," Willie said.

"And I will solve this mystery!"

3. Snow Use

Morning came.

The bell did not ring.

Willie and Slug got up late.

There was a note on the cabin door.

"Maybe it's our first clue," Slug said.

Willie read the note.

Knock knock.

Who's there?

Cargo.

Cargo who?

Car go brummm brummm!

The word *car* was circled.

"Mr. Harry's car!" Willie said.

Willie and Slug ran to the car.

They looked under the seats.

They looked in the trunk.

Nothing.

Mr. Harry blew the whistle.

"You shouldn't be here," he said.

"Follow me."

They followed Mr. Harry.

"Ah, nature," Mr. Harry said.

He put his hand on his heart.

He looked up at the mountains.

"We will walk by the singing birds.

We will walk by the tree toads.

Right, campers?"

There was no answer.

Willie and Slug were gone.

They had already walked by Mr. Harry.

The next day there was another note.

Knock knock.

Who's there?

Avery.

Avery who?

Avery body out of the swimming pool.

The word *swimming* was circled.

"Let's go!" Slug yelled.

"Get your swimming trunks."

"No time," Willie said.

They ran all the way to the pool.

They looked on the diving board.

They looked under the rafts.

Nothing.

Crow stood beside the pool.

"Knock knock," he called to Willie.

"Who's there?" Willie yelled.

"Snow."

"Snow who?"

"Snow use! You'll never find it!"

Crow laughed and laughed.

"Knock knock," Willie said.

"Who's there?" Crow called back.

"Abby."

"Abby who?" Crow said.

He looked bored.

"Abby is on your head!"

Crow yelled and swatted the bee.

He jumped into the pool with a splash.

It was Willie's turn to laugh.

4. Up a Tree

The next day there was another note.

Willie took the note and read it.

Knock knock.

Who's there?

Rocky.

Rocky who?

Rocky-bye baby in the treetop.

"*Tree* is circled," said Willie.

They ran outside to the first tree.

Willie and Slug climbed up.

They looked on every branch.

They looked behind every leaf.

Nothing.

Crow walked up to the tree.

"Knock knock," he called.

"Who's there?" Willie asked.

"Who."

"Who who?" Willie said.

"Willie is an owl!" Crow yelled.

Crow laughed, but Willie did not.

"I am tired of your clues," he said.

The last day of camp came.

"If we don't find it today," Willie said,

"I will never get my book back."

A note flew though the window.

"Another clue," Slug said.

"It's our last chance," Willie said.

They opened the note.

Knock knock.

Who's there?

Ellie.

Ellie who?

Ellie-phant.

"Elephant?" Willie said.

"What kind of clue is that?" Slug said.

"There are no elephants at camp."

"Think about elephants," Willie said.

"Elephants are gray," said Slug.

"They're big," Willie said.

"Elephants have trunks," said Slug.

"Wait!" Willie shouted.

"Get all the clues! I have an idea."

Willie lined up the clues.

"*Car, swimming, tree,* and *elephant.*

What do all these things have?"

"Trunks!" they yelled together.

Slug looked down at Willie's trunk.

"Have you opened your trunk?"

Willie looked at his dirty clothes.

He shook his head.

They opened the trunk.

There was the knock-knock book.

It was right on the clean clothes.

They ran all the way to Crow's cabin.

"Knock knock!" Willie called.

"Who's there?" Crow asked.

"Justin."

"Justin who?"

"Justin time, we found it!"

5. Tootle-oo!

"I still have a problem," said Willie.

He looked in his trunk.

He saw all his clean clothes.

"I forgot to change my clothes.

My mother will be mad."

"No problem," said Slug.

He yelled for all the campers.

Everyone put on Willie's clothes.

Too big or too small didn't matter.

They played in the clothes.

Soon all the clothes were dirty.

They put them back in the trunk.

When the parents came,

Willie's mother was proud.

"You changed your clothes this year!"

Willie smiled.

Slug's father was proud.

"You read this whole book."

Slug smiled.

"And you," Crow's mother said.

"Is that cherry pie on your chin?"

Crow did not smile.

Mr. Harry blew the whistle.

"Another week of camp is over.

Ah, nature!" he said.

He put his hand on his heart.

He looked up at the mountains.

"We will miss the singing of the birds.

We will miss the call of the tree toad.

Right, campers?" he asked.

There was no answer.

The campers were already missing.

They were going home.

Willie saw Crow in the parking lot.

"Crow!" Willie said. "You have—"

"Only talk in jokes," Crow said.

"But, Crow!"

"Jokes," Crow said.

"Knock knock."

"Who's there?"

"Teresa."

"Teresa who?"

"Teresa bee on your head again!"

Crow swatted the bee.

He ran for the pool.

Willie and Slug laughed.

"Knock knock," Willie said to Slug.

"Who's there?"

"Tootle."

"Tootle who?"

"Tootle-oo to you too, for this year!"

About the Author

Betsy Duffey is the author of more than a dozen popular books for young readers. She grew up in Morgantown, West Virginia, and spent many happy summer weeks at Camp Horseshoe in Elkins, West Virginia. She now lives in Atlanta with her husband and two sons.

About the Illustrator

Fiona Dunbar grew up in England, where she has illustrated many books for children and written three of her own. In 1993 she moved to New York, where she now lives with her husband and their daughter, Helena.

THE CAMP KNOCK KNOCK MYSTERY

A Yearling First Choice Chapter Book